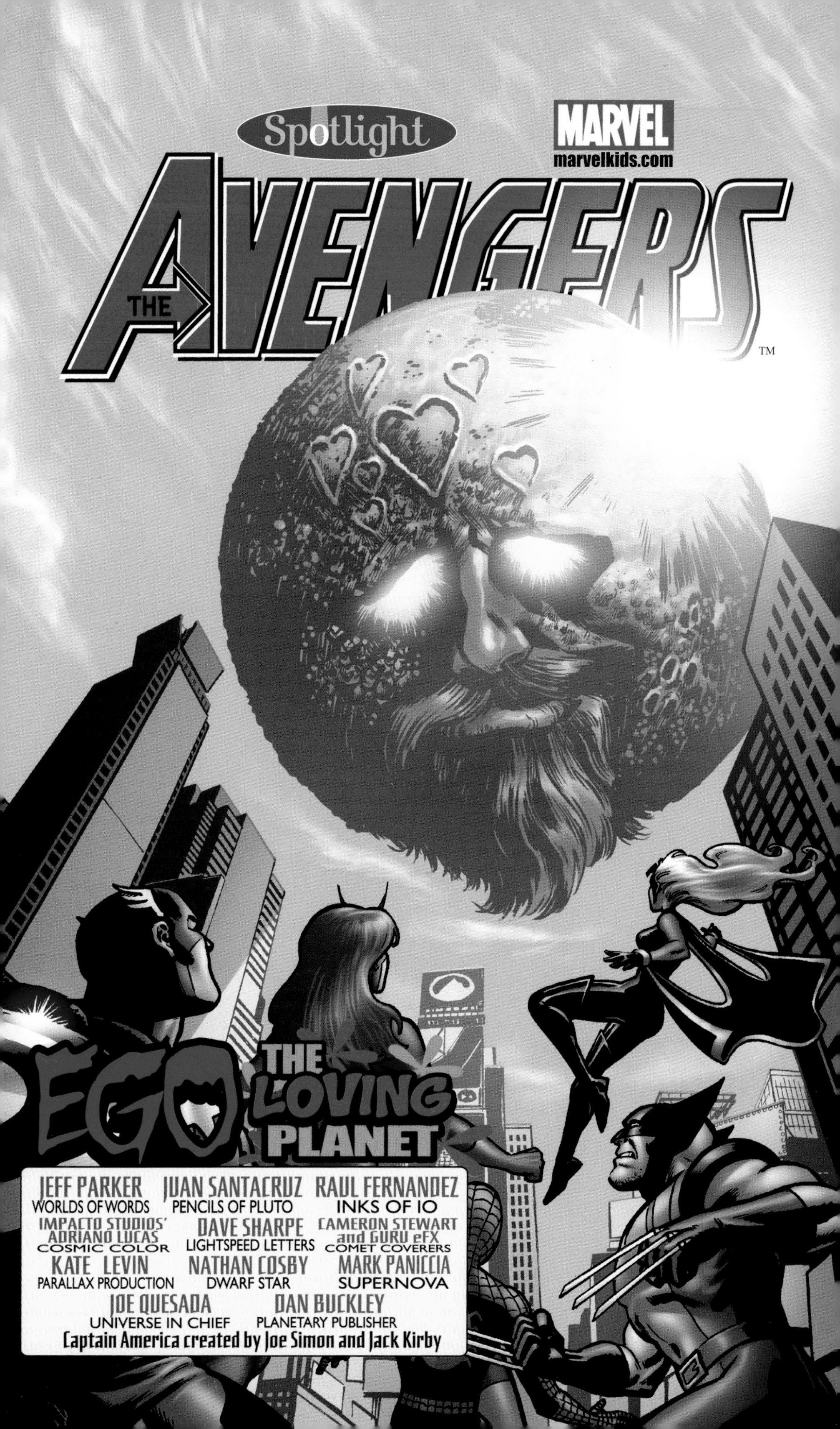
Spotlight
MARVEL
marvelkids.com
THE AVENGERS
TM
EGO THE LOVING PLANET
JEFF PARKER WORLDS OF WORDS
JUAN SANTACRUZ PENCILS OF PLUTO
RAUL FERNANDEZ INKS OF IO
IMPACTO STUDIOS' ADRIANO LUCAS COSMIC COLOR
DAVE SHARPE LIGHTSPEED LETTERS
CAMERON STEWART and GURU eFX COMET COVERERS
KATE LEVIN PARALLAX PRODUCTION
NATHAN COSBY DWARF STAR
MARK PANICCIA SUPERNOVA
JOE QUESADA UNIVERSE IN CHIEF
DAN BUCKLEY PLANETARY PUBLISHER
Captain America created by Joe Simon and Jack Kirby

visit us at www.abdopublishing.com

Reinforced library bound edition published in 2013 by Spotlight, a division
of the ABDO Group, 8000 West 78th Street, Edina, Minnesota 55439.
Spotlight produces high-quality reinforced library bound editions for schools
and libraries. Published by agreement with Marvel Entertainment, LLC.
The stories, characters, and incidents mentioned are entirely fictional.
All rights reserved. Used under authorization.

Printed in the United States of America, North Mankato, Minnesota.
052012
092012
♻ This book contains at least 10% recycled materials.

marvelkids.com

TM & © 2012 Marvel & Subs.

Library of Congress Cataloging-in-Publication Data

Parker, Jeff, 1966-
  Ego : the loving planet / story by Jeff Parker ; art by Juan Santacruz. --
Reinforced library bound ed.
      p. cm. -- (Avengers)
  "Marvel."
  Summary: A planet-sized entity that has achieved consciousness will
devastate Earth unless the Avengers can stop it.
  ISBN 978-1-61479-014-3
  1. Graphic novels. [1. Graphic novels. 2. Superheroes--Fiction. 3. Planets--
Fiction.] I. Santacruz, Juan, ill. II. Title.
  PZ7.7.P252Ego 2012
  741.5'973--dc23
                                    2012000926

ISBN 978-1-61479-014-3 (reinforced library edition)

All Spotlight books are reinforced library binding
and manufactured in the United States of America.

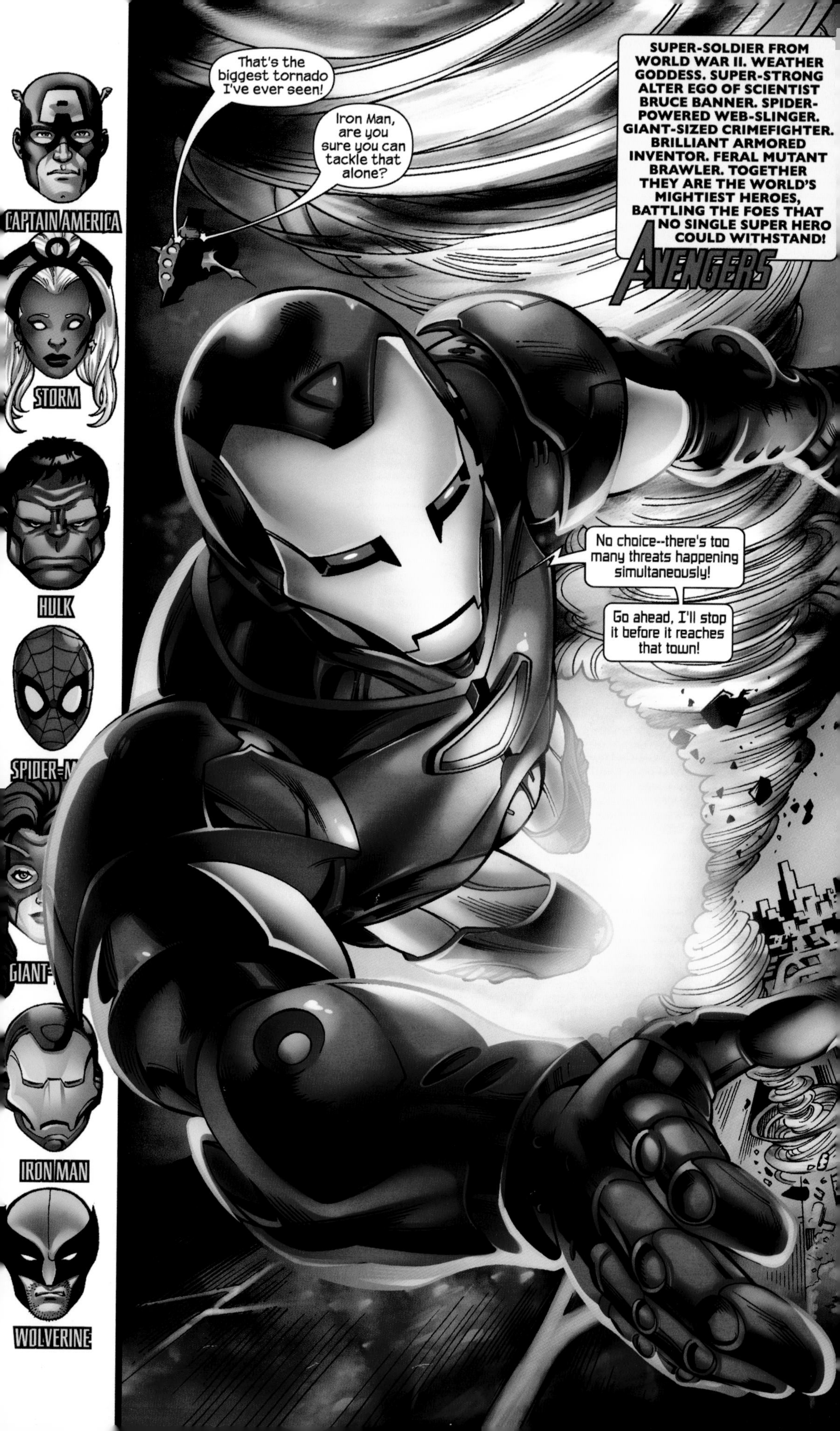
CAPTAIN AMERICA
STORM
HULK
SPIDER-M
GIANT-
IRON MAN
WOLVERINE
That's the biggest tornado I've ever seen!
Iron Man, are you sure you can tackle that alone?
SUPER-SOLDIER FROM WORLD WAR II. WEATHER GODDESS. SUPER-STRONG ALTER EGO OF SCIENTIST BRUCE BANNER. SPIDER-POWERED WEB-SLINGER. GIANT-SIZED CRIMEFIGHTER. BRILLIANT ARMORED INVENTOR. FERAL MUTANT BRAWLER. TOGETHER THEY ARE THE WORLD'S MIGHTIEST HEROES, BATTLING THE FOES THAT NO SINGLE SUPER HERO COULD WITHSTAND!
AVENGERS
No choice--there's too many threats happening simultaneously!
Go ahead, I'll stop it before it reaches that town!

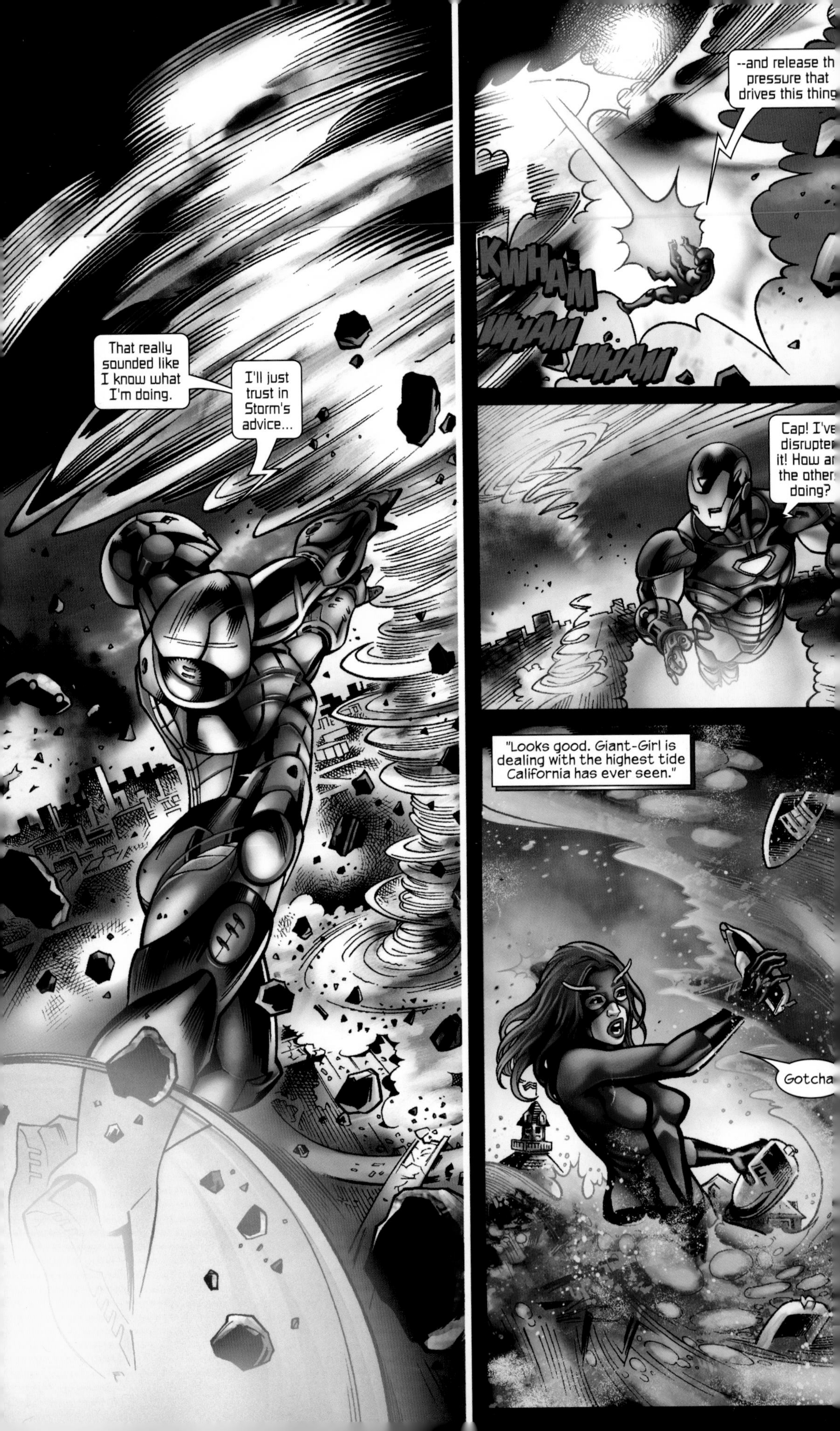
That really sounded like I know what I'm doing.
I'll just trust in Storm's advice...
--and release th
pressure that
drives this thing
KWHAM
WHAM
WHAM
Cap! I've disrupte
it! How ar
the other
doing?
"Looks good. Giant-Girl is dealing with the highest tide California has ever seen."
Gotcha

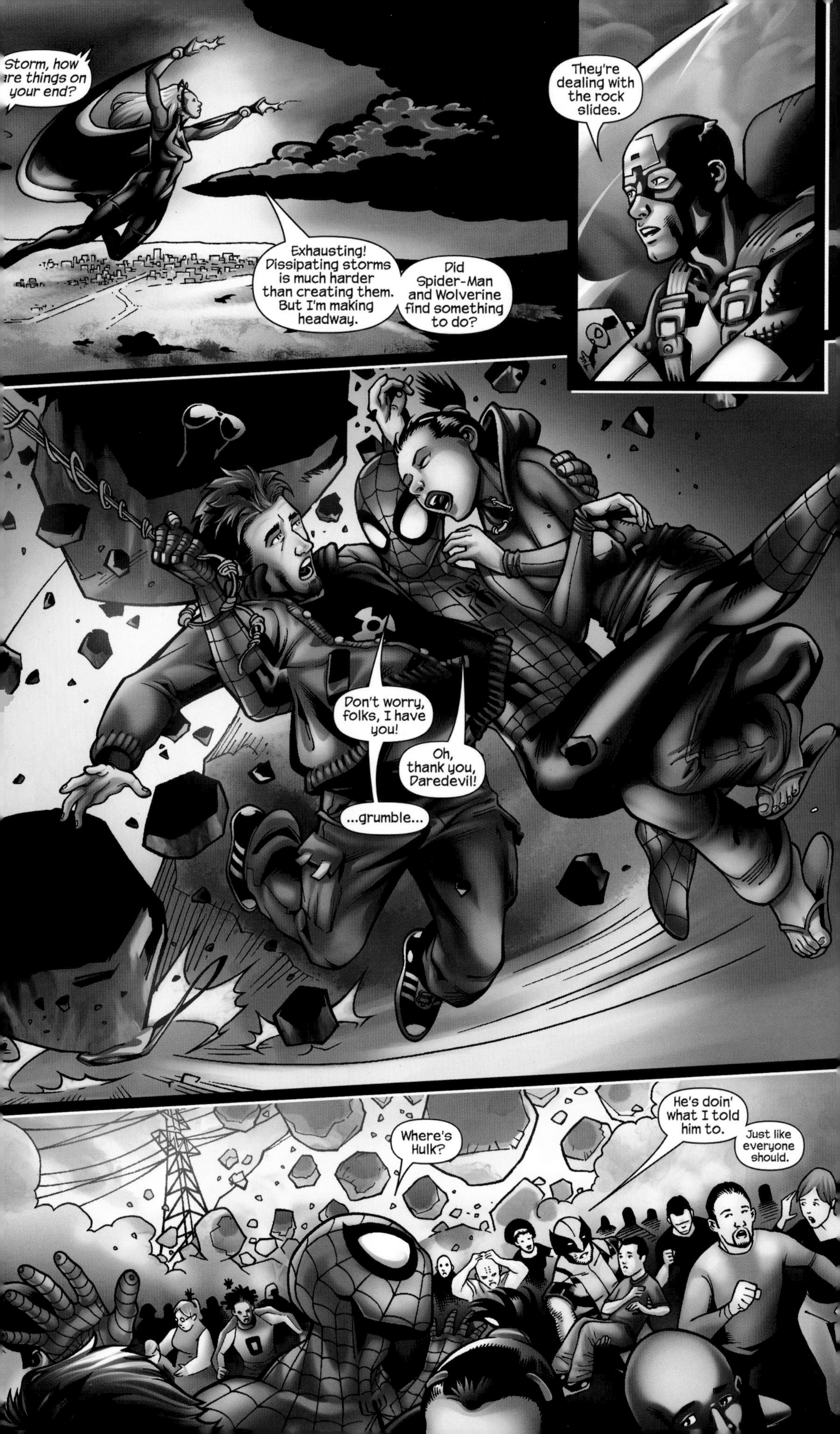
Storm, how are things on your end?
Exhausting! Dissipating storms is much harder than creating them. But I'm making headway.
Did Spider-Man and Wolverine find something to do?
They're dealing with the rock slides.
Don't worry, folks, I have you!
Oh, thank you, Daredevil!
...grumble...
Where's Hulk?
He's doin' what I told him to.
Just like everyone should.

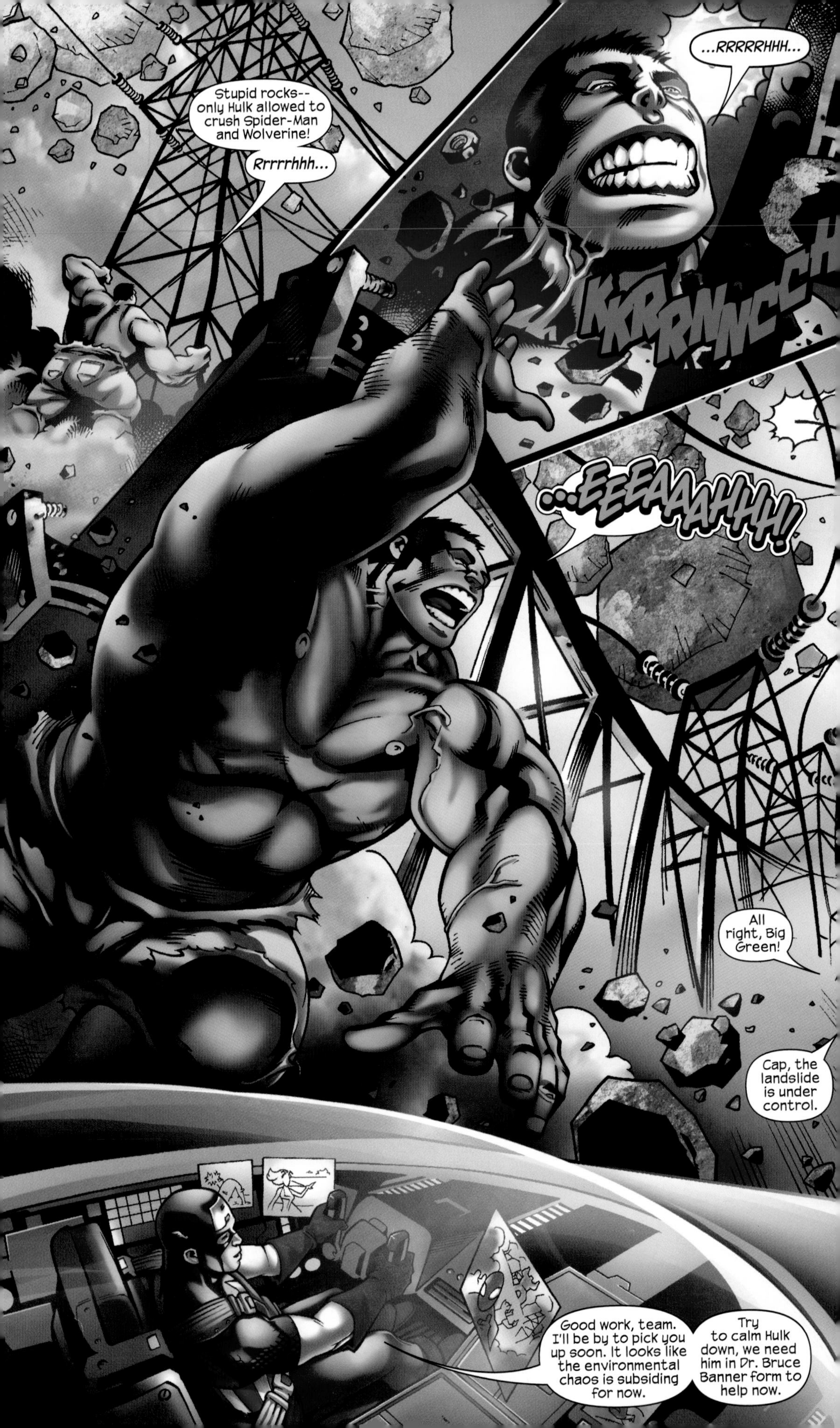
Stupid rocks--
only Hulk allowed to
crush Spider-Man
and Wolverine!
Rrrrrhhh...
...RRRRRHHH...
KKRRRNNCCH
...EEEAAAHHHH!
All right, Big Green!
Cap, the landslide is under control.
Good work, team. I'll be by to pick you up soon. It looks like the environmental chaos is subsiding for now.
Try to calm Hulk down, we need him in Dr. Bruce Banner form to help now.

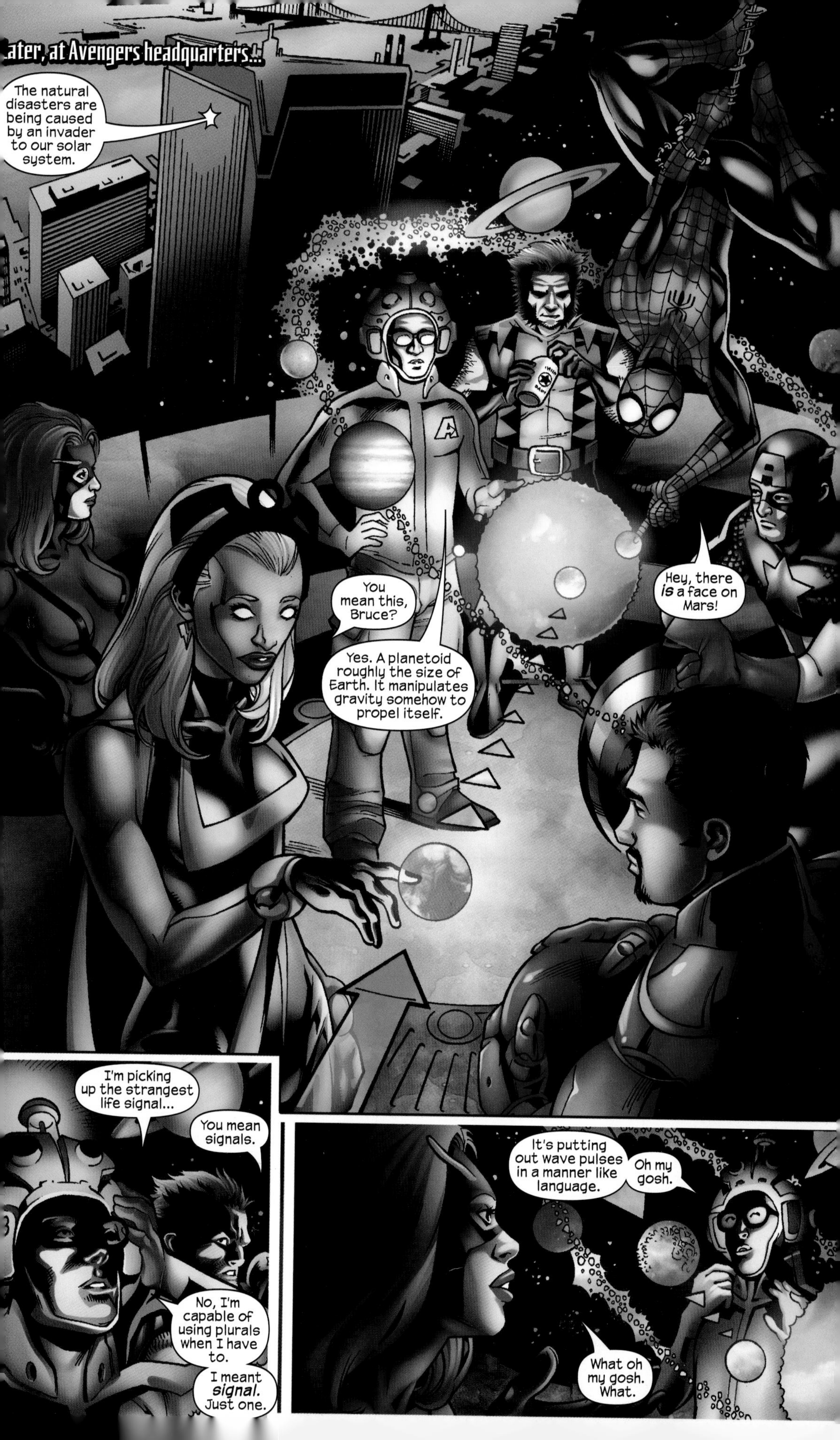

ater, at Avengers headquarters...
The natural disasters are being caused by an invader to our solar system.
You mean this, Bruce?
Yes. A planetoid roughly the size of Earth. It manipulates gravity somehow to propel itself.
Hey, there is a face on Mars!
I'm picking up the strangest life signal...
You mean signals.
No, I'm capable of using plurals when I have to.
I meant signal. Just one.
It's putting out wave pulses in a manner like language.
Oh my gosh.
What oh my gosh. What.

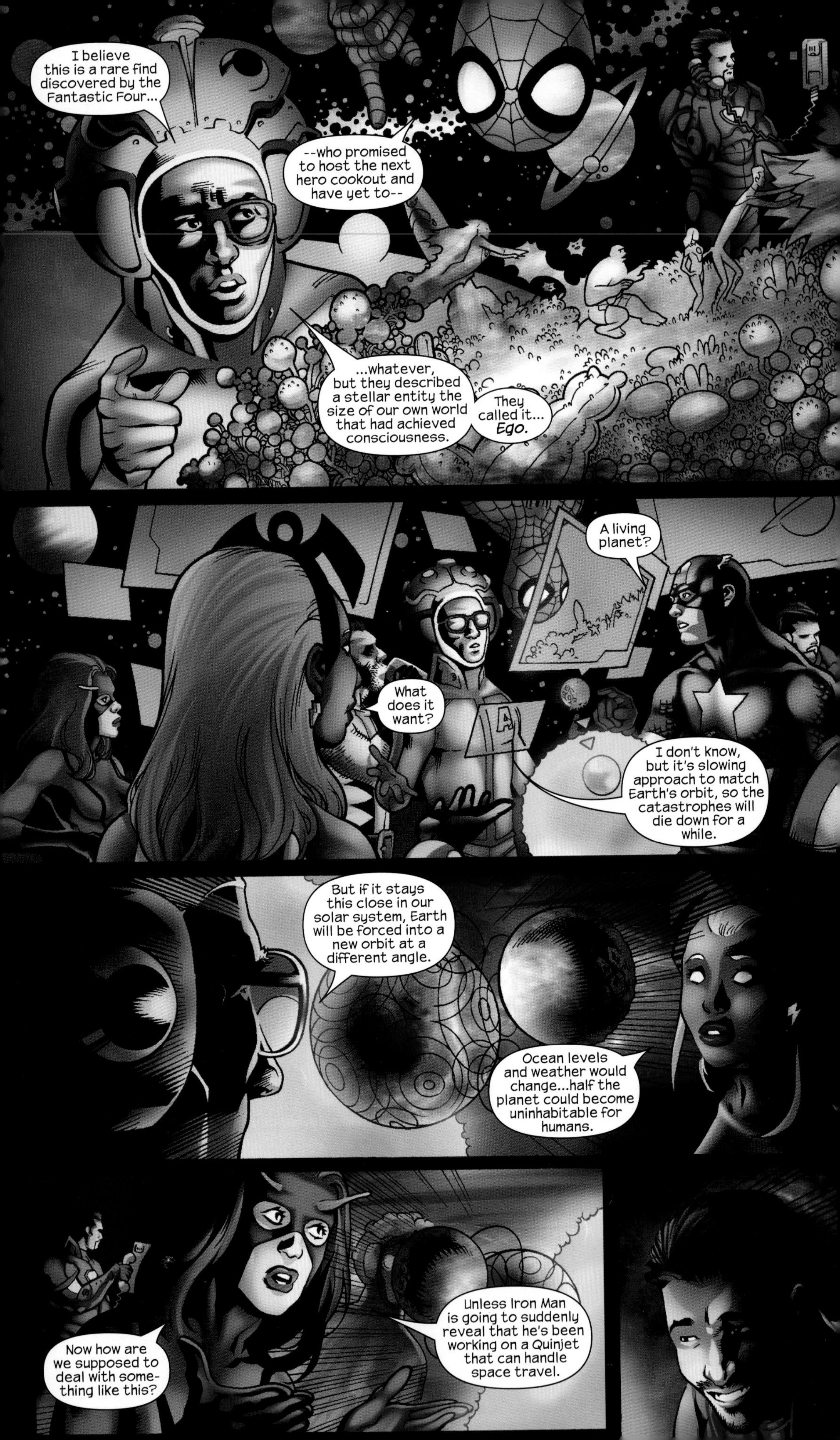
I believe this is a rare find discovered by the Fantastic Four...
--who promised to host the next hero cookout and have yet to--
...whatever, but they described a stellar entity the size of our own world that had achieved consciousness.
They called it... *Ego.*
A living planet?
What does it want?
I don't know, but it's slowing approach to match Earth's orbit, so the catastrophes will die down for a while.
But if it stays this close in our solar system, Earth will be forced into a new orbit at a different angle.
Ocean levels and weather would change...half the planet could become uninhabitable for humans.
Now how are we supposed to deal with some-thing like this?
Unless Iron Man is going to suddenly reveal that he's been working on a Quinjet that can handle space travel.

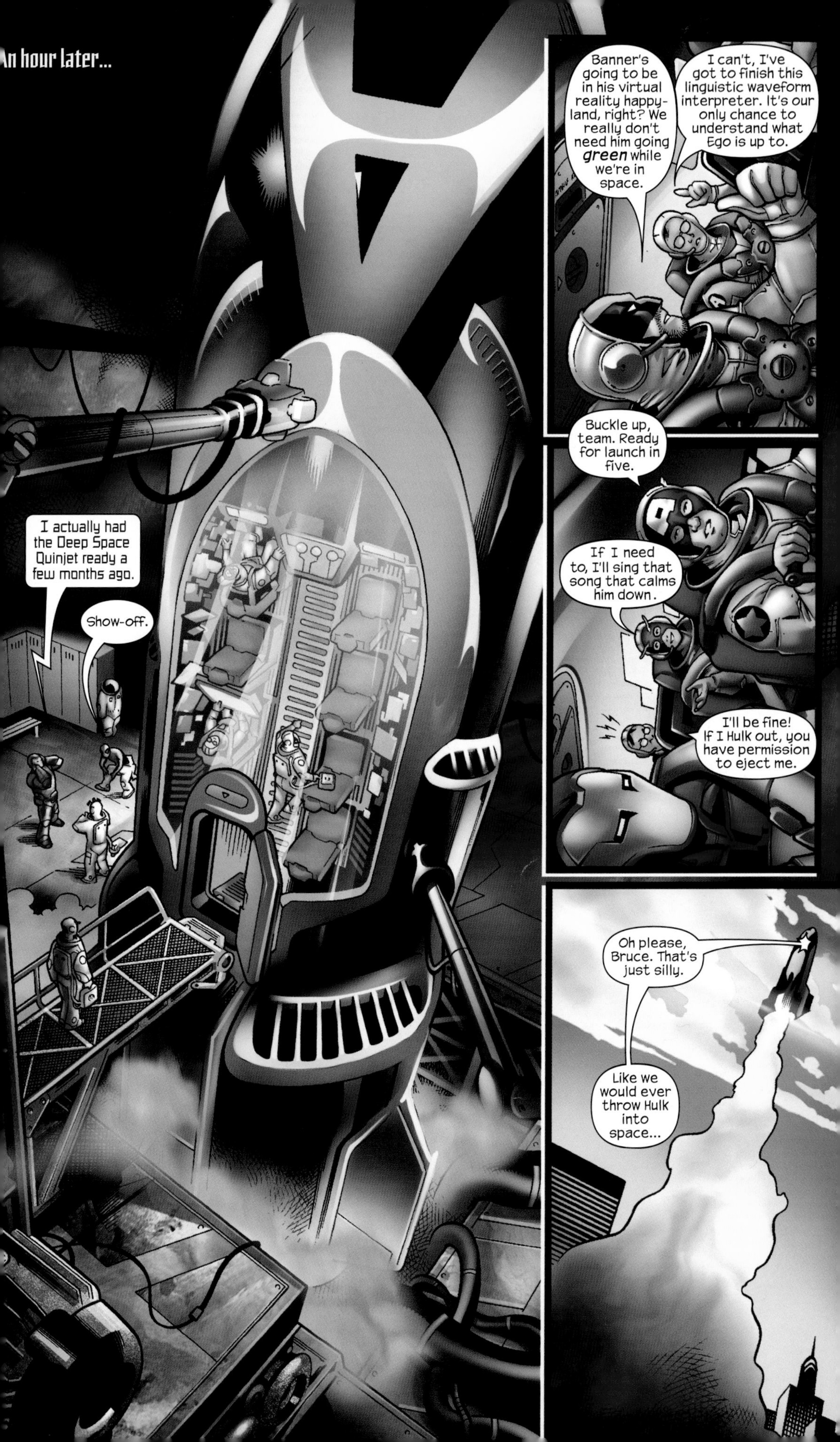
An hour later...
I actually had the Deep Space Quinjet ready a few months ago.
Show-off.
Banner's going to be in his virtual reality happy-land, right? We really don't need him going **green** while we're in space.
I can't, I've got to finish this linguistic waveform interpreter. It's our only chance to understand what Ego is up to.
Buckle up, team. Ready for launch in five.
If I need to, I'll sing that song that calms him down.
I'll be fine! If I Hulk out, you have permission to eject me.
Oh please, Bruce. That's just silly.
Like we would ever throw Hulk into space...

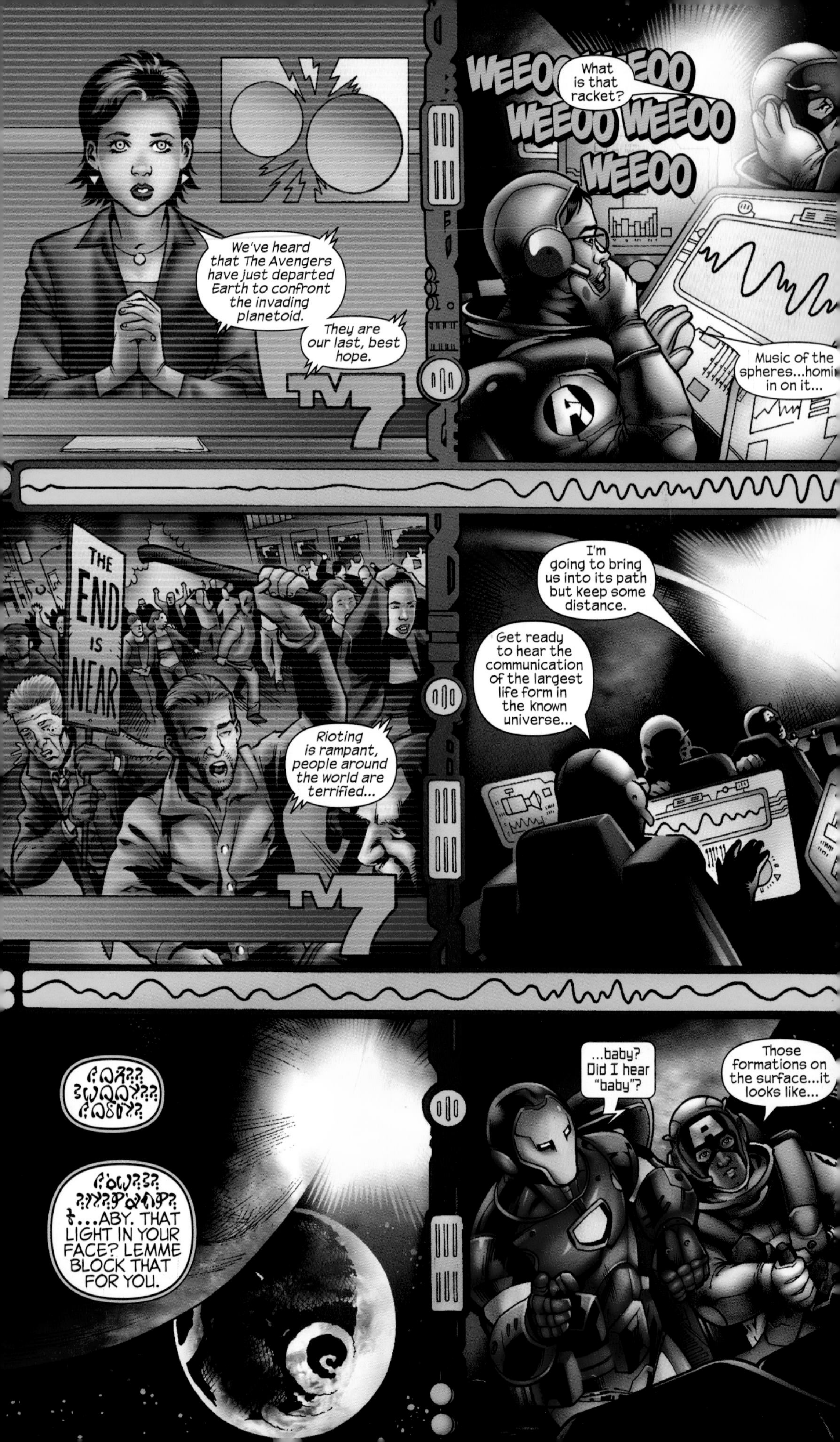
We've heard that The Avengers have just departed Earth to confront the invading planetoid.
They are our last, best hope.
TV7
What is that racket?
WEEOO WEEOO
WEEOO
Music of the spheres...homi in on it...
THE END IS NEAR
Rioting is rampant, people around the world are terrified...
TV7
I'm going to bring us into its path but keep some distance.
Get ready to hear the communication of the largest life form in the known universe...
...ABY. THAT LIGHT IN YOUR FACE? LEMME BLOCK THAT FOR YOU.
...baby? Did I hear "baby"?
Those formations on the surface...it looks like...

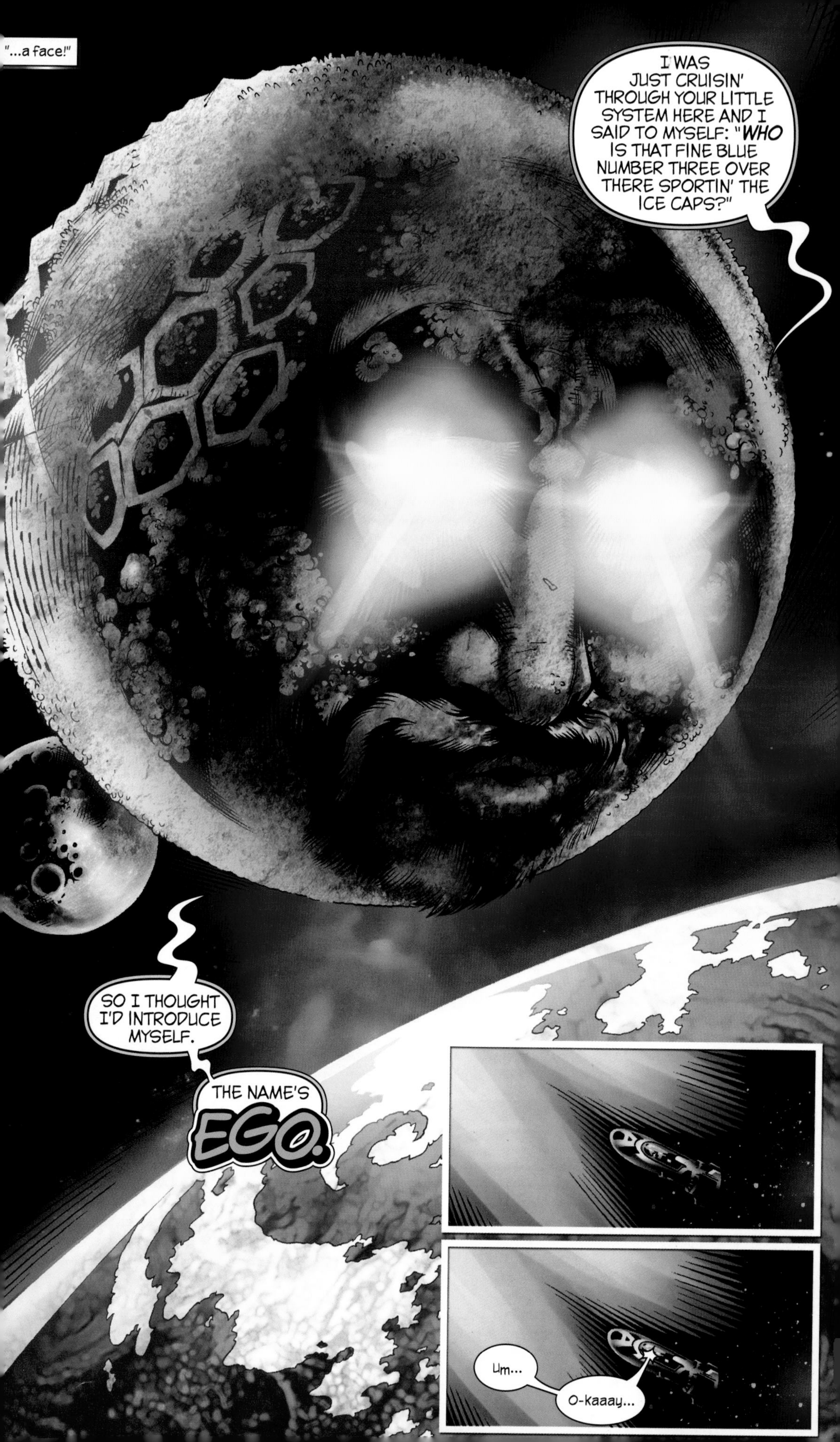
"...a face!"
I WAS JUST CRUISIN' THROUGH YOUR LITTLE SYSTEM HERE AND I SAID TO MYSELF: "WHO IS THAT FINE BLUE NUMBER THREE OVER THERE SPORTIN' THE ICE CAPS?"
SO I THOUGHT I'D INTRODUCE MYSELF.
THE NAME'S EGO.
Um...
O-kaaay...

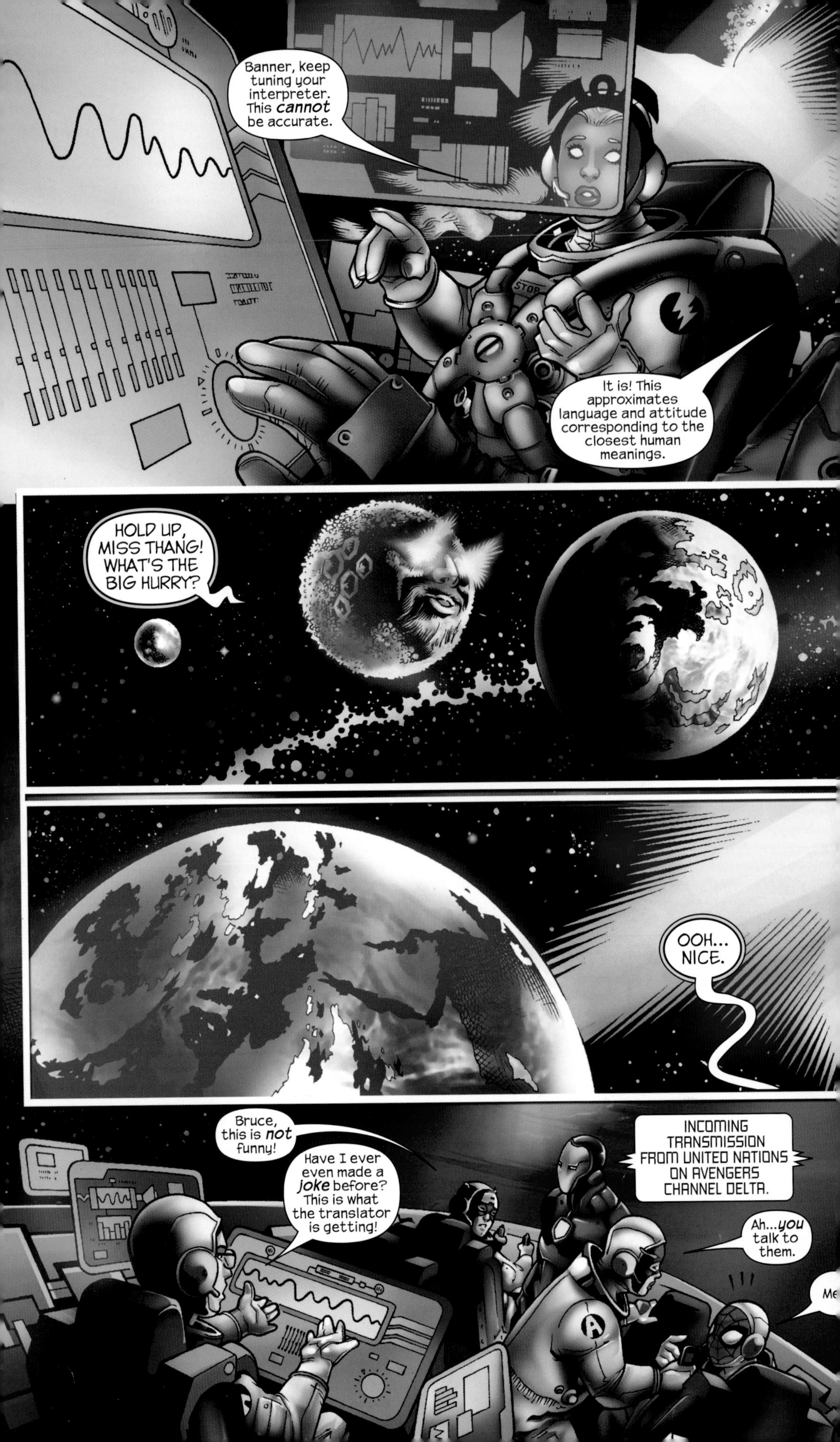
Banner, keep tuning your interpreter. This *cannot* be accurate.
It is! This approximates language and attitude corresponding to the closest human meanings.
HOLD UP, MISS THANG! WHAT'S THE BIG HURRY?
OOH... NICE.
Bruce, this is *not* funny!
Have I ever even made a *joke* before? This is what the translator is getting!
INCOMING TRANSMISSION FROM UNITED NATIONS ON AVENGERS CHANNEL DELTA.
Ah...*you* talk to them.
Me

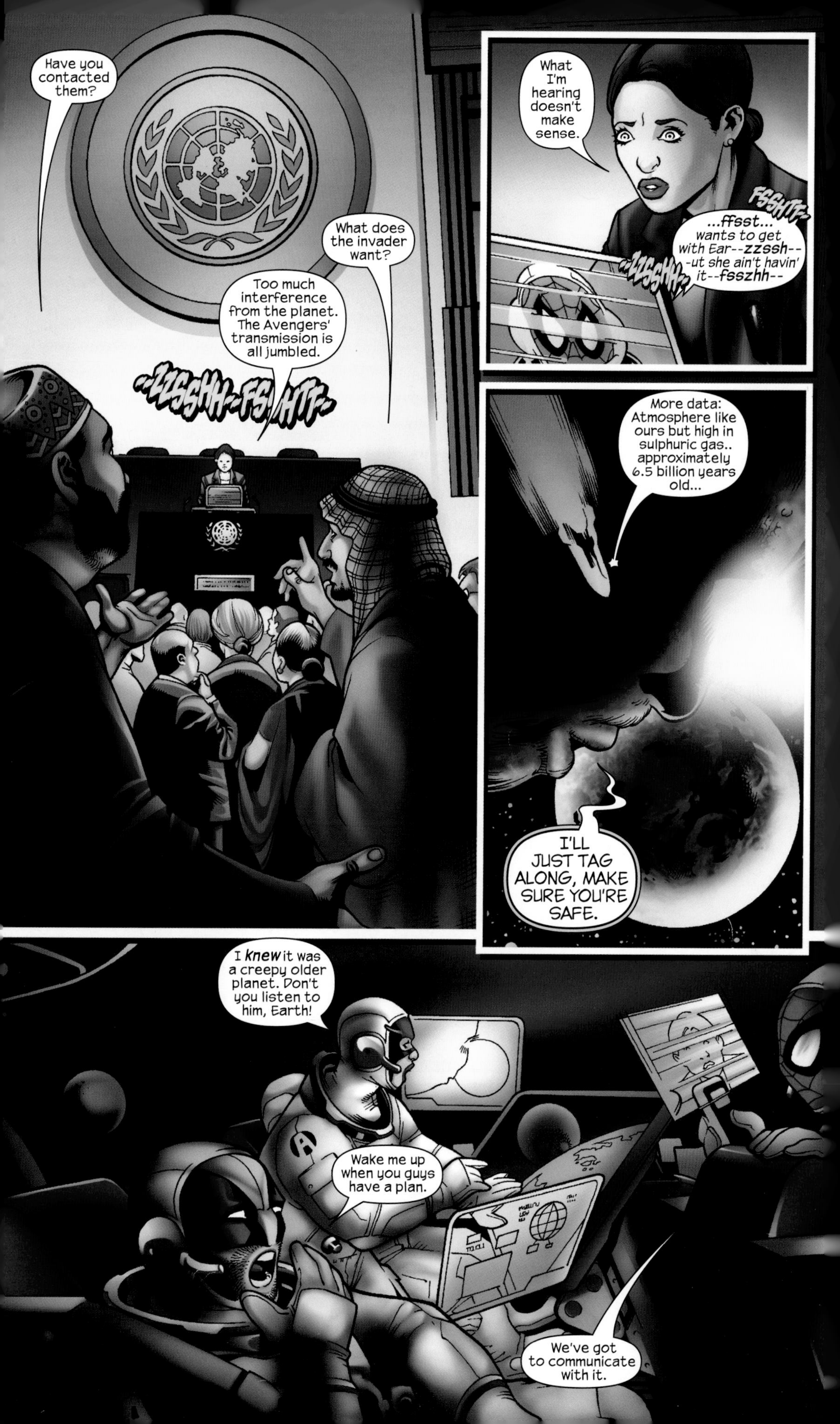
Have you contacted them?
What I'm hearing doesn't make sense.
FSSHTT
...ffsst... wants to get with Ear--zzssh-- -ut she ain't havin' it--fsszhh--
ZZSSHH
What does the invader want?
Too much interference from the planet. The Avengers' transmission is all jumbled.
--ZZSSHH--FSSHTT--
More data: Atmosphere like ours but high in sulphuric gas.. approximately 6.5 billion years old...
I'LL JUST TAG ALONG, MAKE SURE YOU'RE SAFE.
I knew it was a creepy older planet. Don't you listen to him, Earth!
Wake me up when you guys have a plan.
We've got to communicate with it.

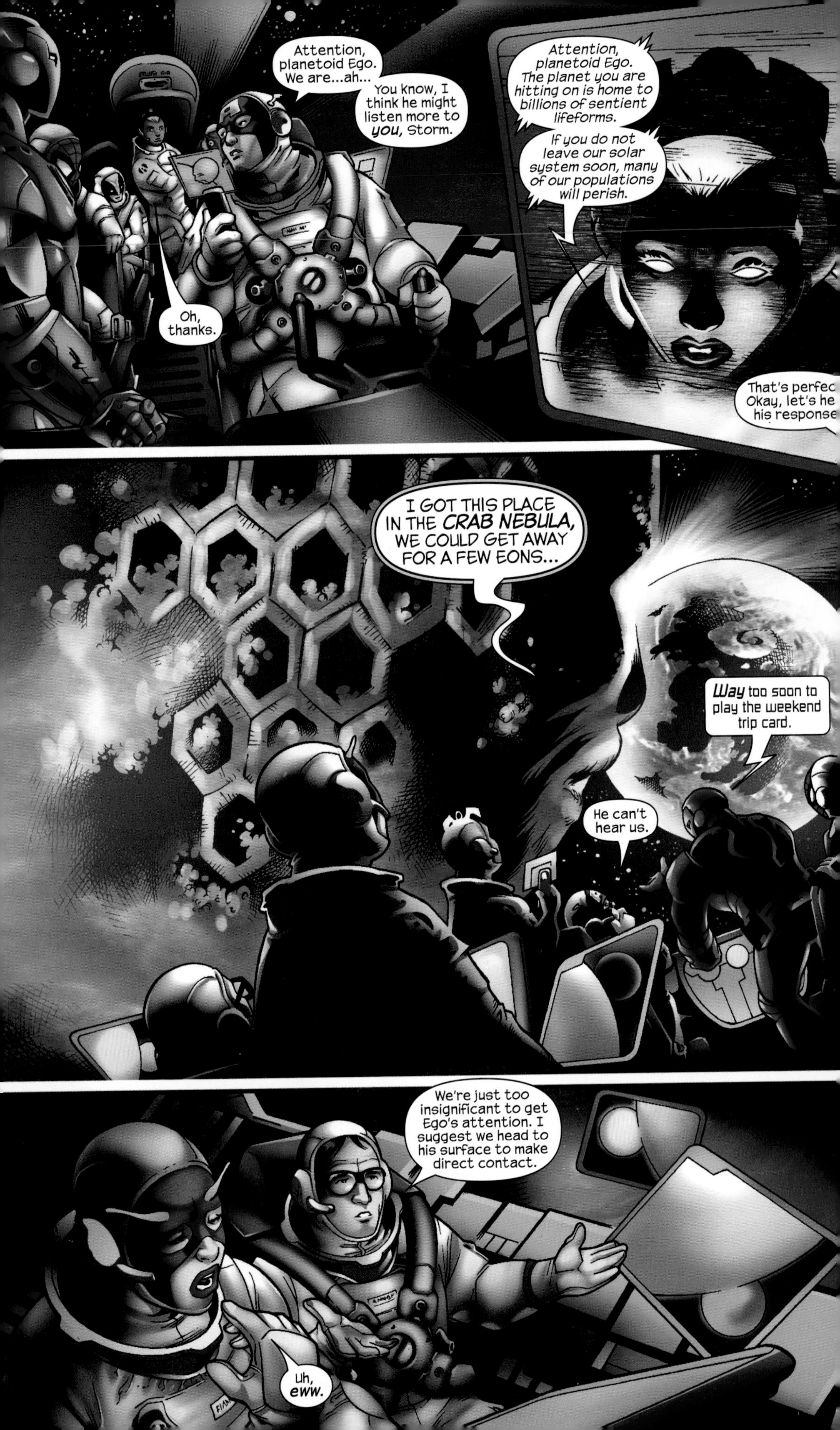
Attention, planetoid Ego. We are...ah...
You know, I think he might listen more to *you*, Storm.
Oh, thanks.
Attention, planetoid Ego. The planet you are hitting on is home to billions of sentient lifeforms.
If you do not leave our solar system soon, many of our populations will perish.
That's perfec Okay, let's he his response
I GOT THIS PLACE IN THE *CRAB NEBULA,* WE COULD GET AWAY FOR A FEW EONS...
Way too soon to play the weekend trip card.
He can't hear us.
We're just too insignificant to get Ego's attention. I suggest we head to his surface to make direct contact.
Uh, *eww.*

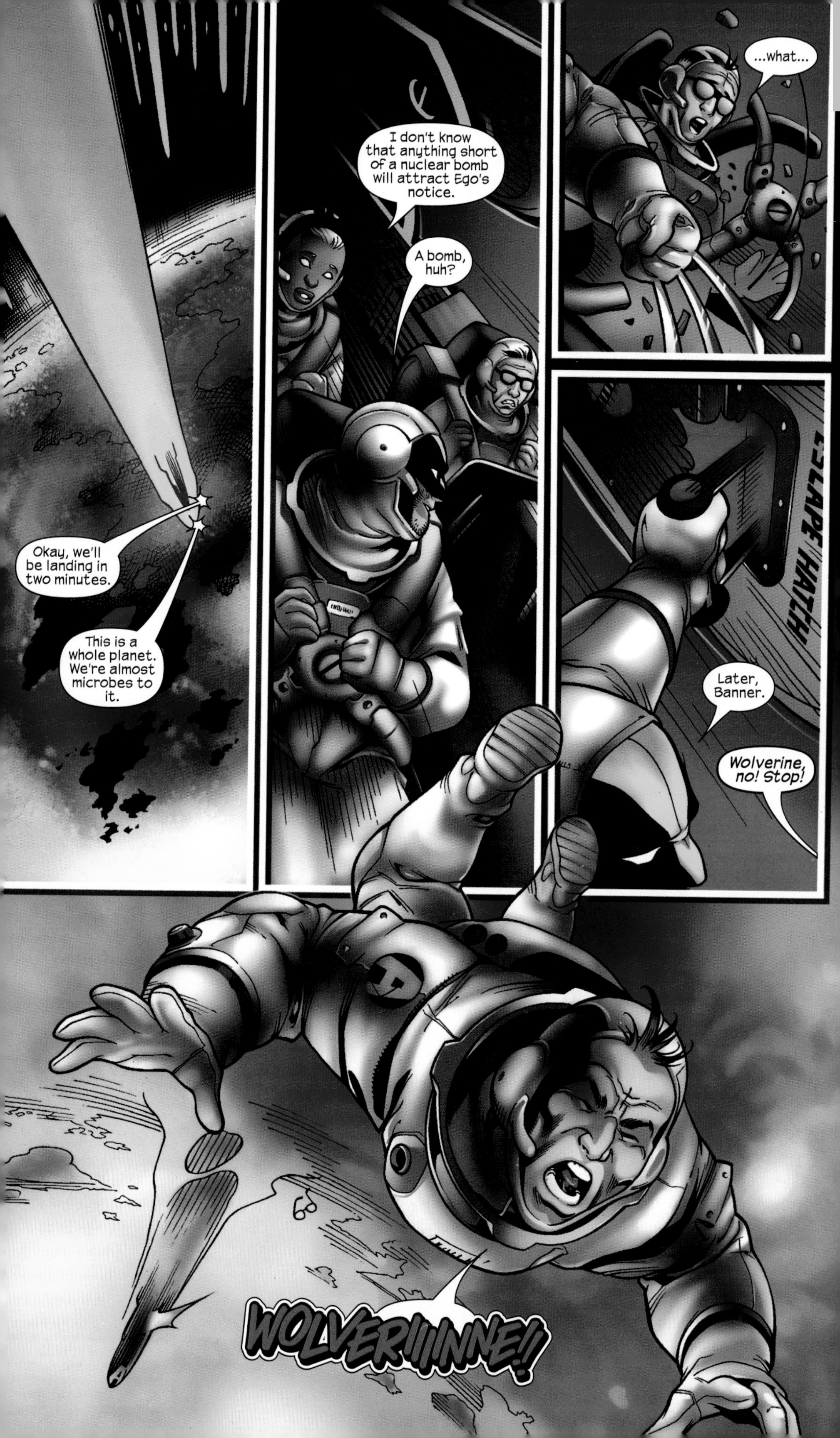
Okay, we'll be landing in two minutes.
This is a whole planet. We're almost microbes to it.
I don't know that anything short of a nuclear bomb will attract Ego's notice.
A bomb, huh?
...what...
ESCAPE HATCH
Later, Banner.
Wolverine, no! Stop!
WOLVERIIIINNE!!

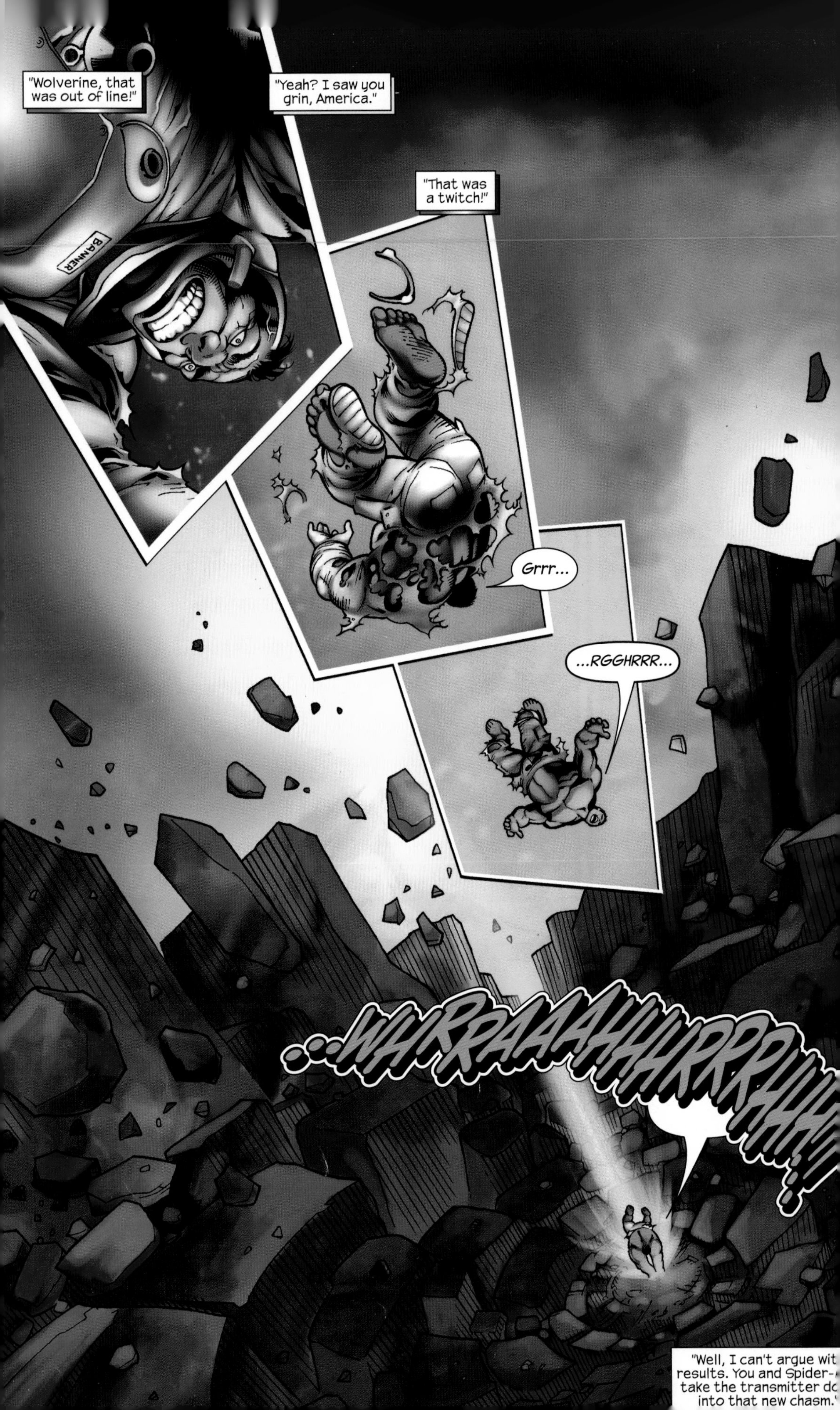

"Wolverine, that was out of line!"
"Yeah? I saw you grin, America."
"That was a twitch!"
BANNER
Grrr...
...RGGHRRR...
...WHRRAAAAHHHRRRHH!
"Well, I can't argue wit results. You and Spider- take the transmitter d into that new chasm.

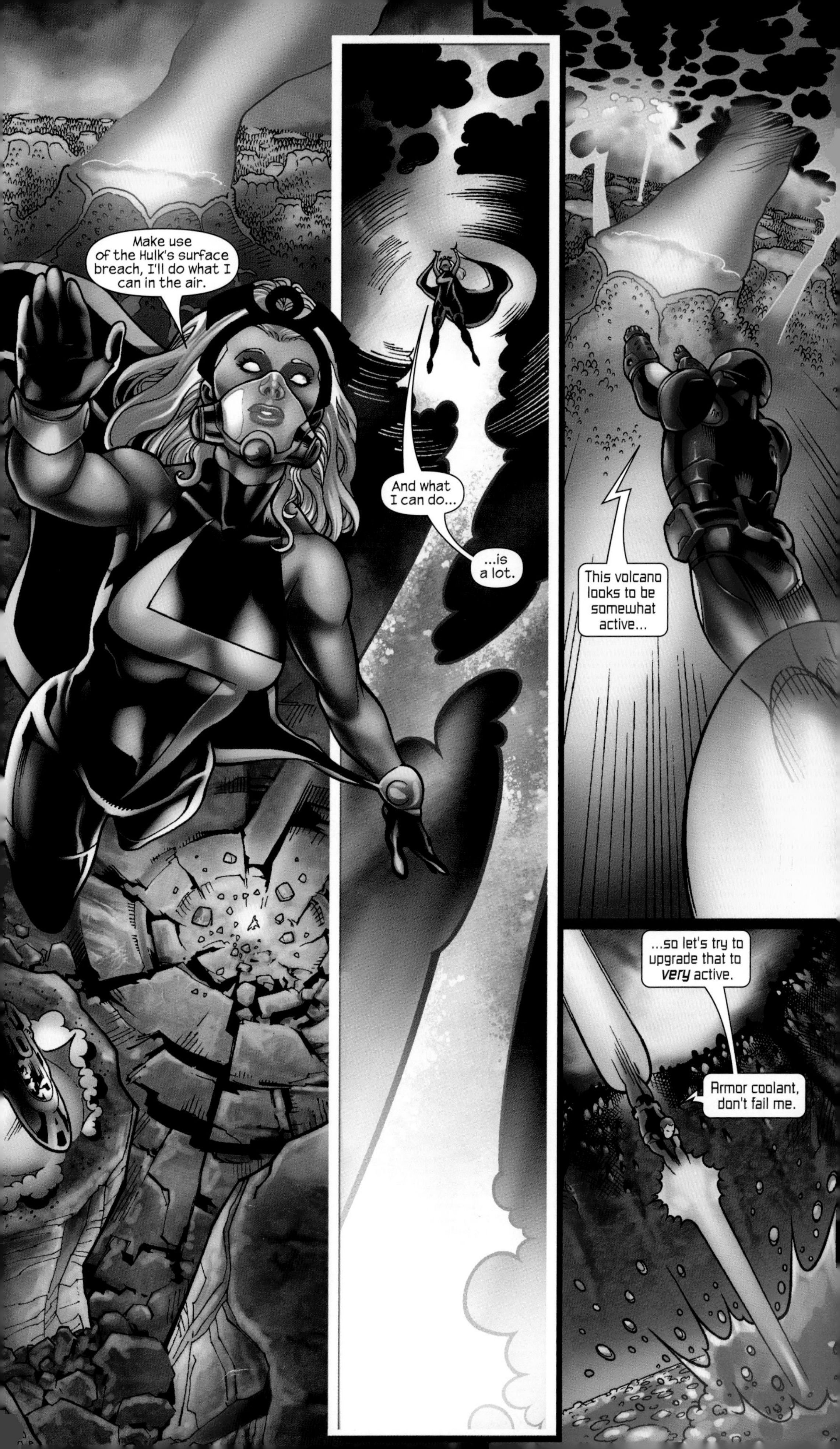

Make use of the Hulk's surface breach, I'll do what I can in the air.
And what I can do...
...is a lot.
This volcano looks to be somewhat active...
...so let's try to upgrade that to *very* active.
Armor coolant, don't fail me.

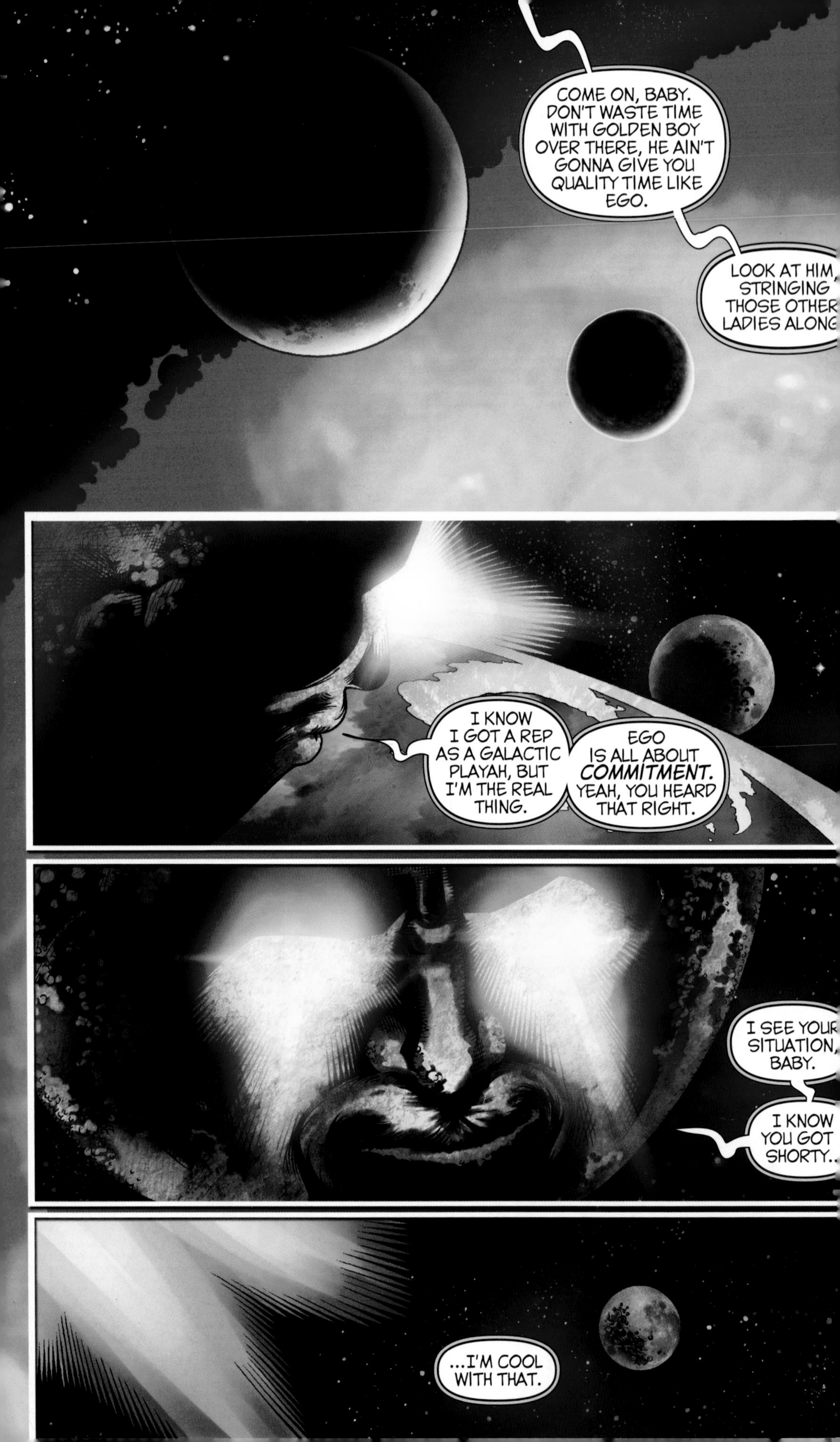
COME ON, BABY. DON'T WASTE TIME WITH GOLDEN BOY OVER THERE, HE AIN'T GONNA GIVE YOU QUALITY TIME LIKE EGO.
LOOK AT HIM, STRINGING THOSE OTHER LADIES ALONG
I KNOW I GOT A REP AS A GALACTIC PLAYAH, BUT I'M THE REAL THING.
EGO IS ALL ABOUT ***COMMITMENT.*** YEAH, YOU HEARD THAT RIGHT.
I SEE YOUR SITUATION, BABY.
I KNOW YOU GOT SHORTY...
...I'M COOL WITH THAT.

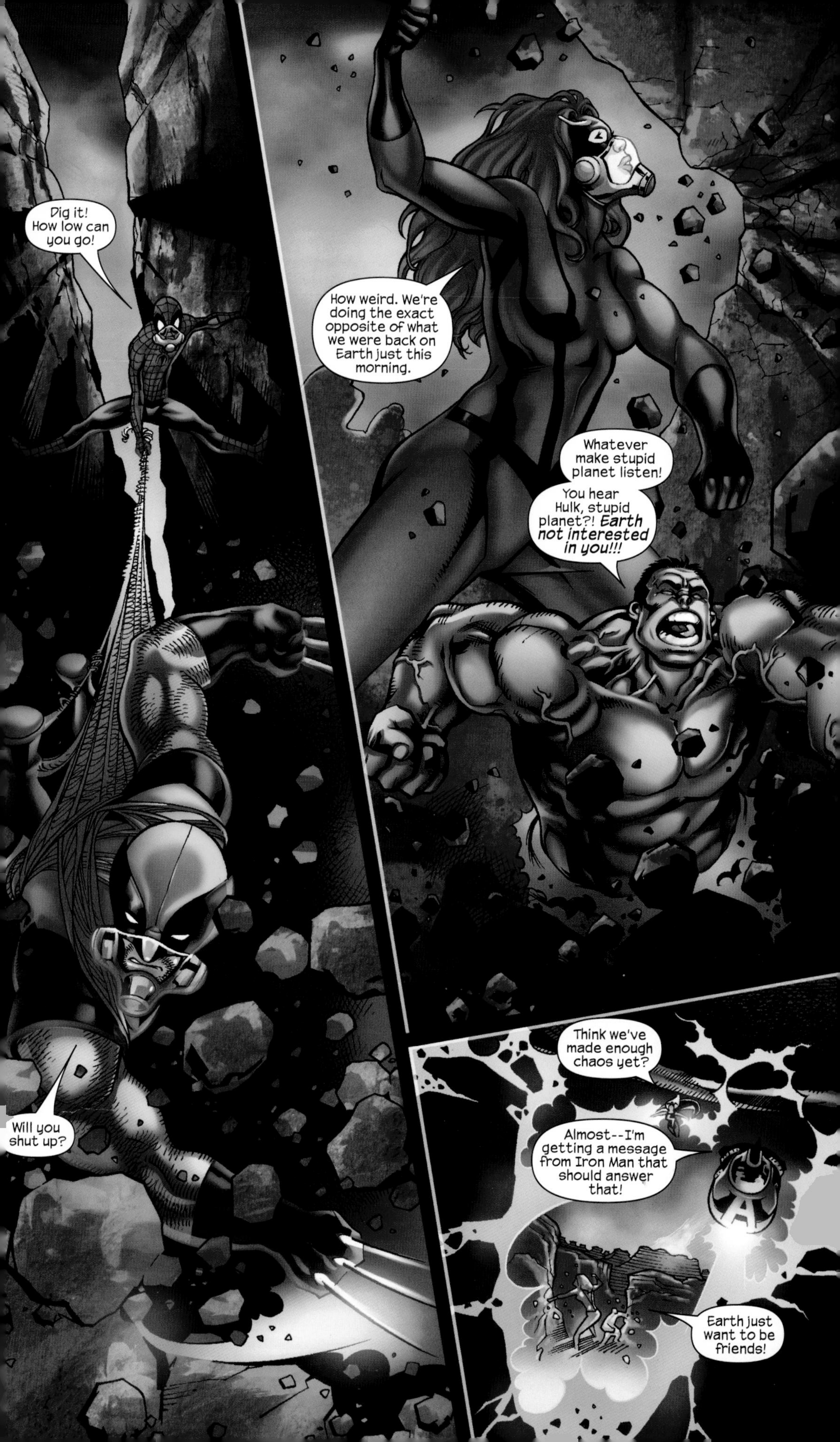
Dig it! How low can you go!
Will you shut up?
How weird. We're doing the exact opposite of what we were back on Earth just this morning.
Whatever make stupid planet listen!
You hear Hulk, stupid planet?! Earth not interested in you!!!
Think we've made enough chaos yet?
Almost--I'm getting a message from Iron Man that should answer that!
Earth just want to be friends!

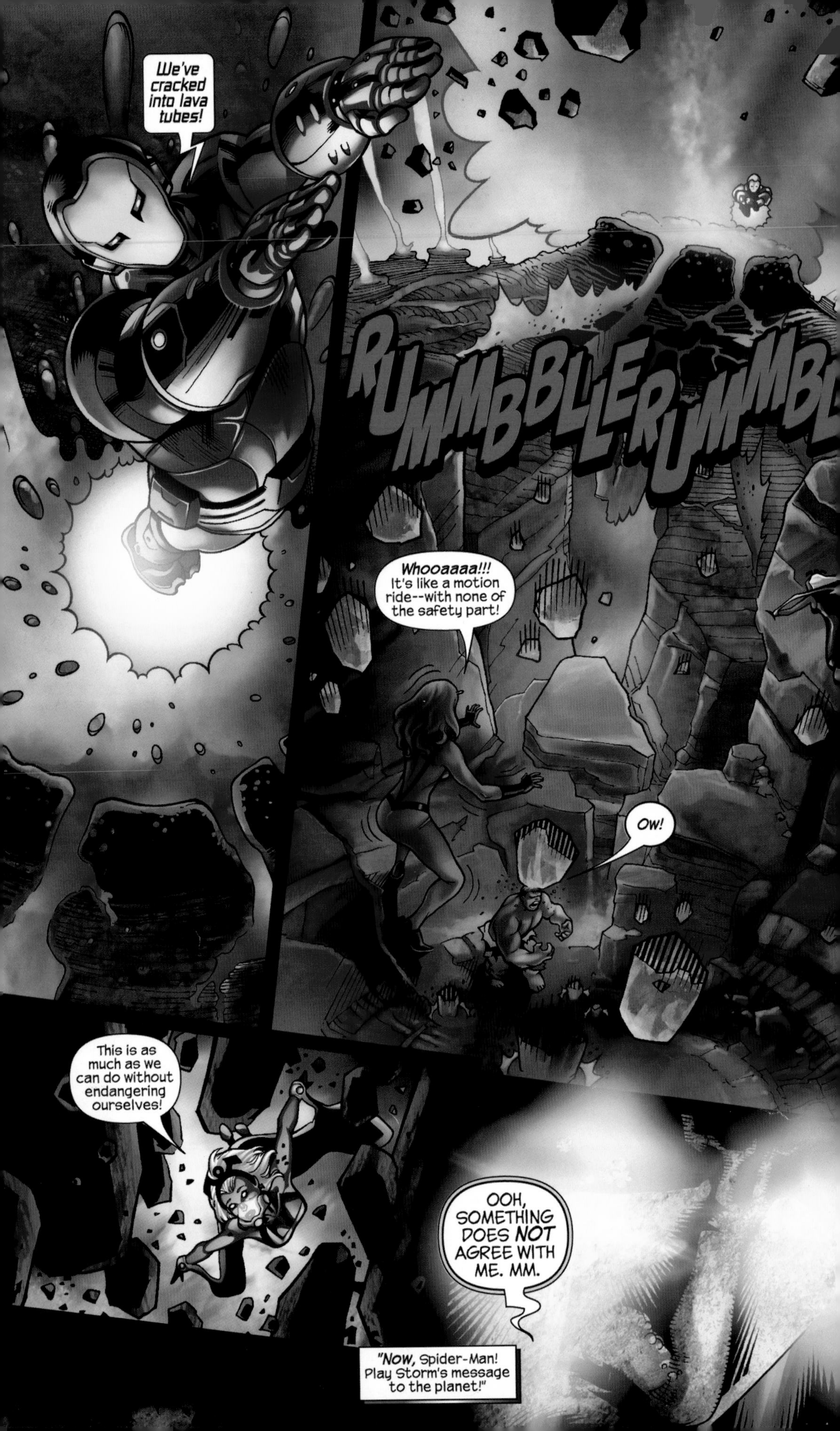
We've cracked into lava tubes!
RUMMBBLLERUMMMBL
Whooaaaa!!! It's like a motion ride--with none of the safety part!
OW!
This is as much as we can do without endangering ourselves!
OOH, SOMETHING DOES NOT AGREE WITH ME. MM.
"NOW, Spider-Man! Play Storm's message to the planet!"

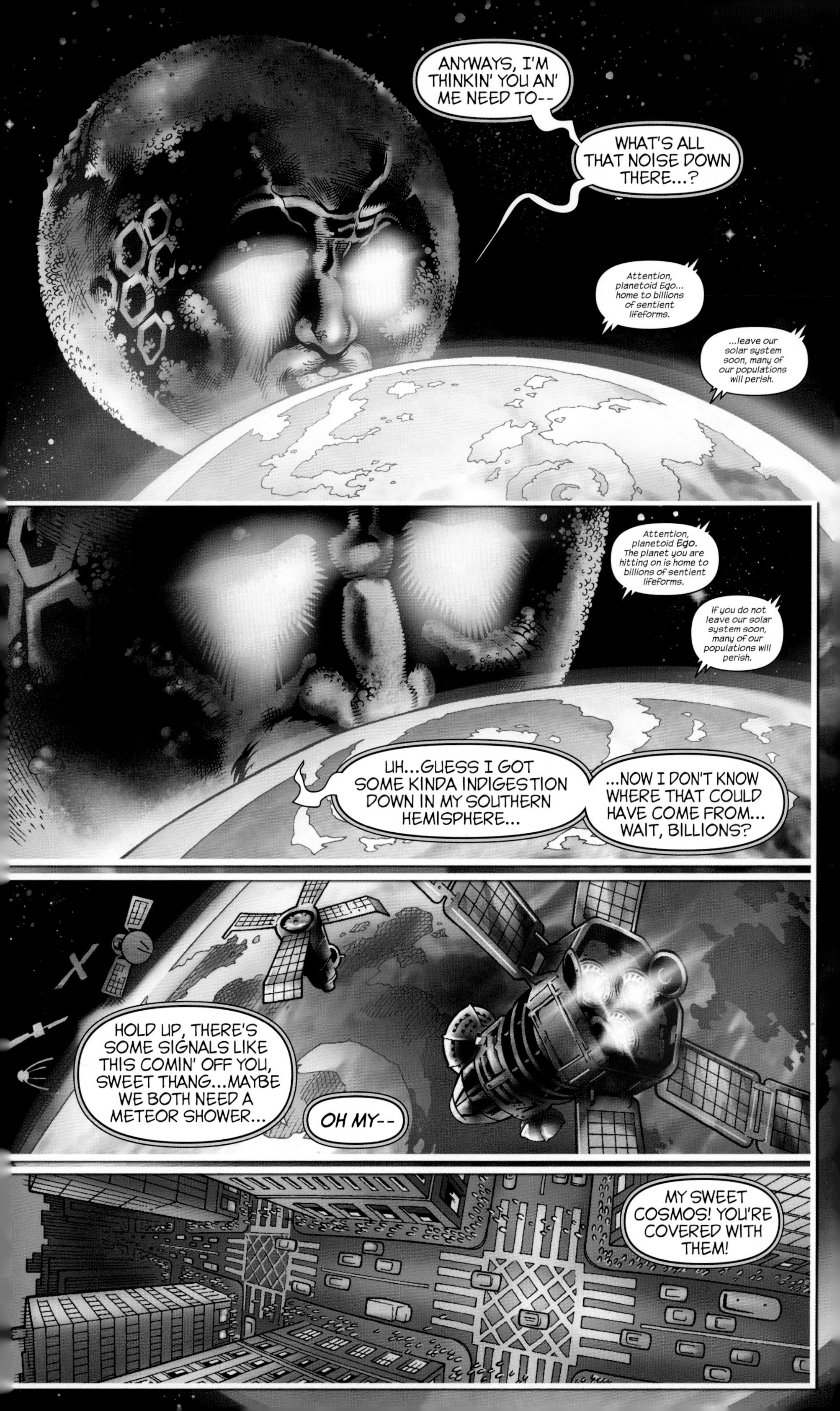

ANYWAYS, I'M THINKIN' YOU AN' ME NEED TO--
WHAT'S ALL THAT NOISE DOWN THERE...?
Attention, planetoid Ego... home to billions of sentient lifeforms.
...leave our solar system soon, many of our populations will perish.
Attention, planetoid Ego. The planet you are hitting on is home to billions of sentient lifeforms.
If you do not leave our solar system soon, many of our populations will perish.
UH...GUESS I GOT SOME KINDA INDIGESTION DOWN IN MY SOUTHERN HEMISPHERE...
...NOW I DON'T KNOW WHERE THAT COULD HAVE COME FROM... WAIT, BILLIONS?
HOLD UP, THERE'S SOME SIGNALS LIKE THIS COMIN' OFF YOU, SWEET THANG...MAYBE WE BOTH NEED A METEOR SHOWER...
OH MY--
MY SWEET COSMOS! YOU'RE COVERED WITH THEM!

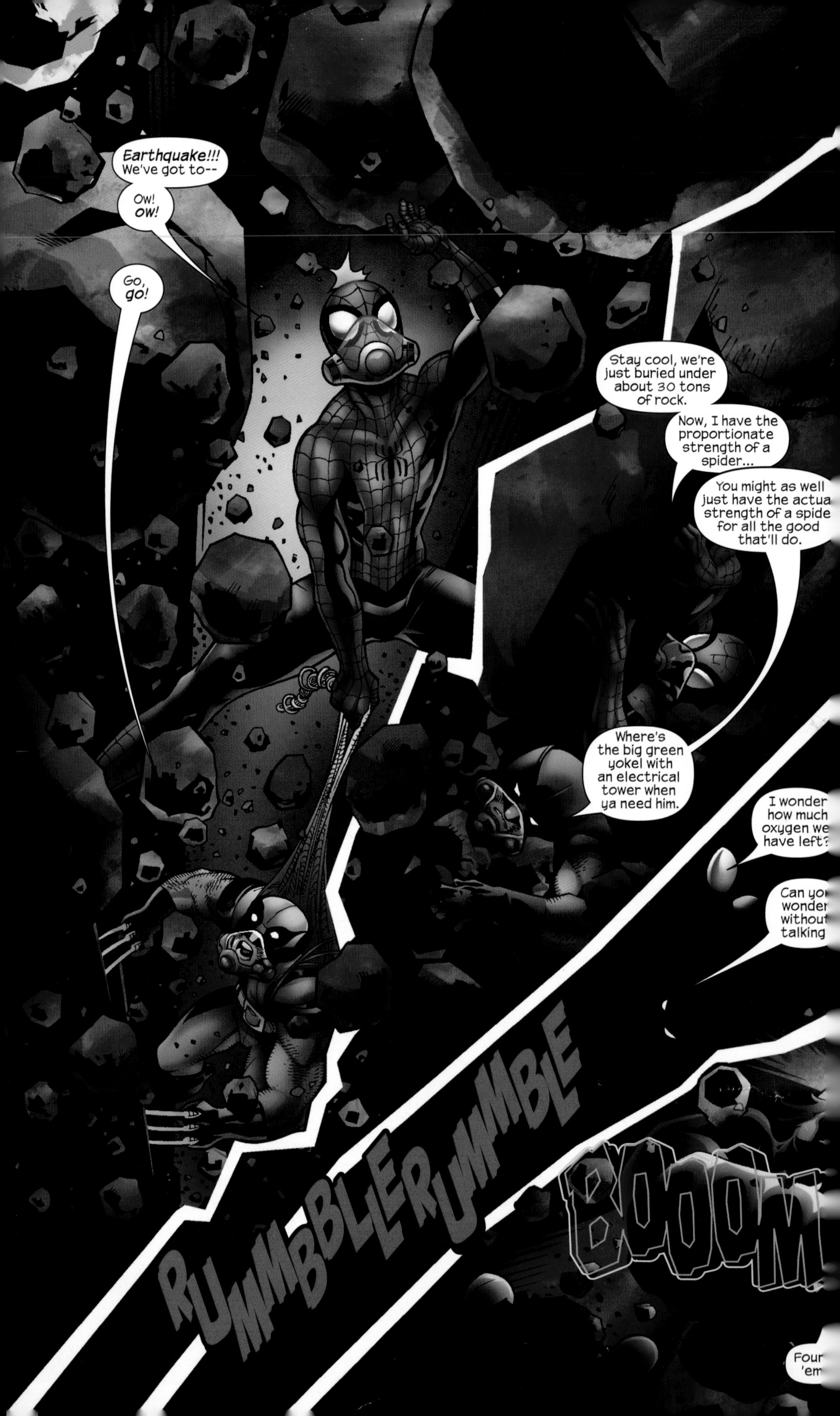
Earthquake!!! We've got to--
Ow! OW!
Go, go!
Stay cool, we're just buried under about 30 tons of rock.
Now, I have the proportionate strength of a spider...
You might as well just have the actua strength of a spide for all the good that'll do.
Where's the big green yokel with an electrical tower when ya need him.
I wonder how much oxygen we have left?
Can yo wonder without talking
RUMMBLLERUMMBLE
BOOOM
Four 'em

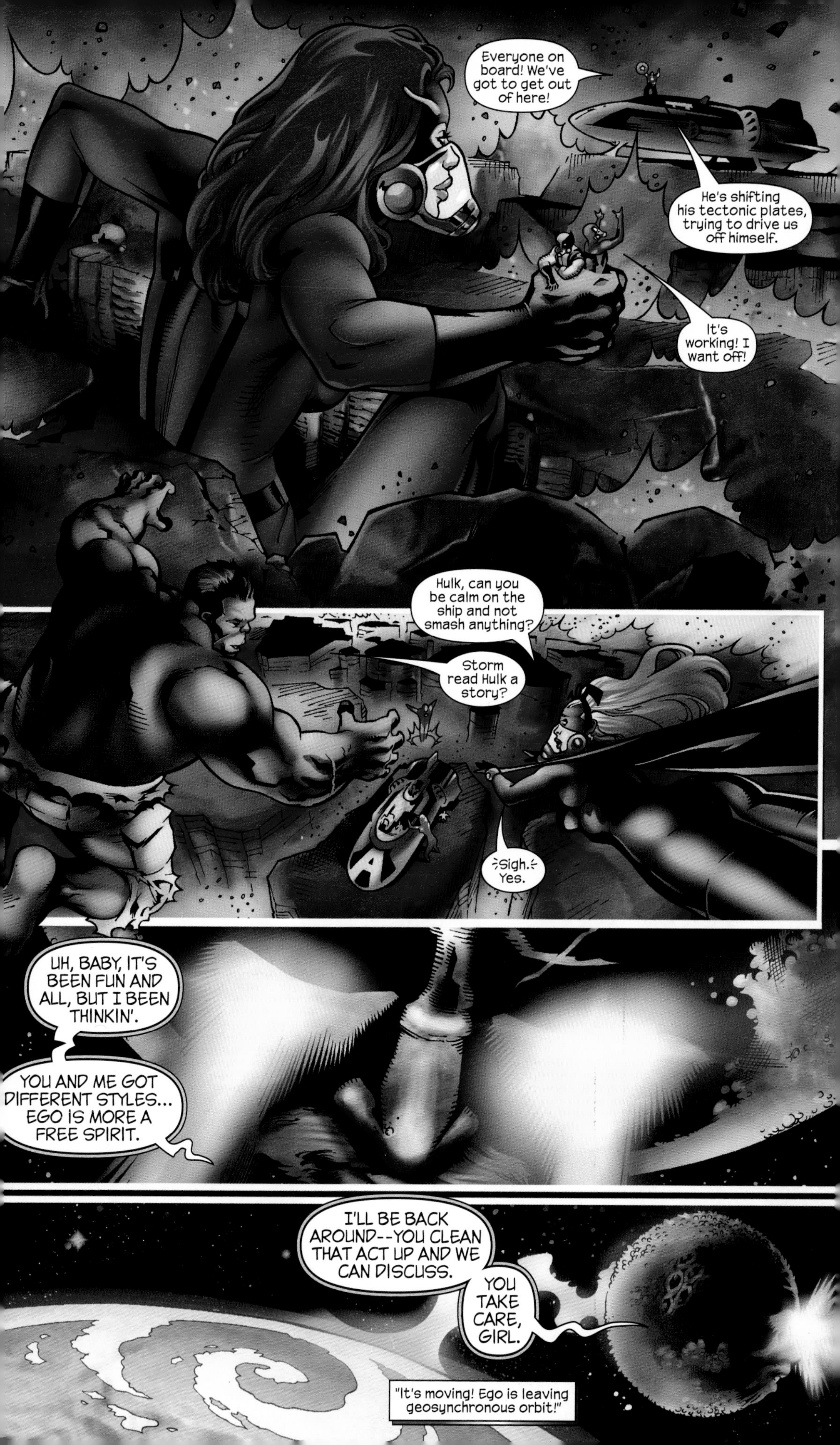
Everyone on board! We've got to get out of here!
He's shifting his tectonic plates, trying to drive us off himself.
It's working! I want off!
Hulk, can you be calm on the ship and not smash anything?
Storm read Hulk a story?
Sigh. Yes.
UH, BABY, IT'S BEEN FUN AND ALL, BUT I BEEN THINKIN'.
YOU AND ME GOT DIFFERENT STYLES... EGO IS MORE A FREE SPIRIT.
I'LL BE BACK AROUND--YOU CLEAN THAT ACT UP AND WE CAN DISCUSS.
YOU TAKE CARE, GIRL.
"It's moving! Ego is leaving geosynchronous orbit!"

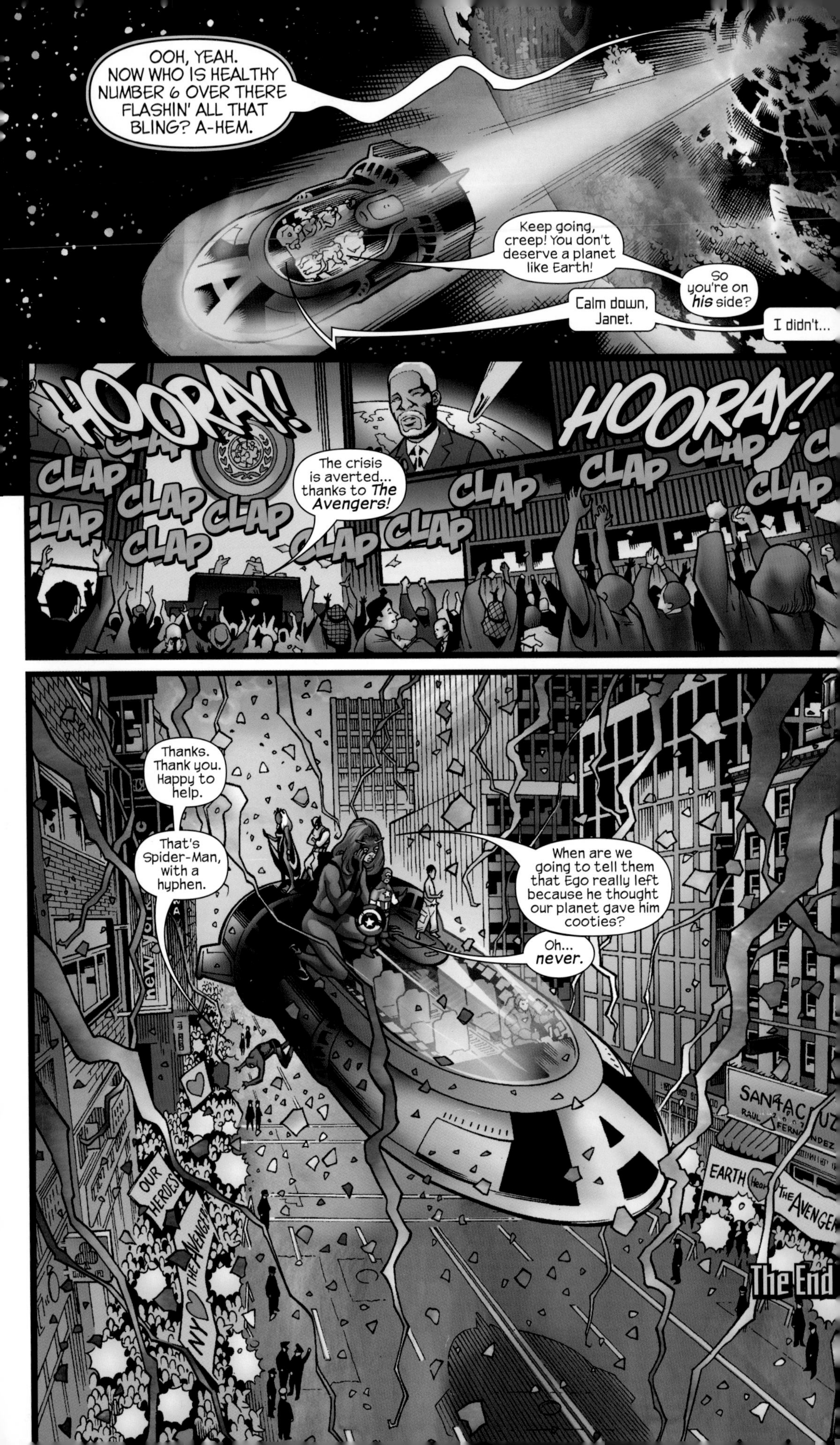
OOH, YEAH. NOW WHO IS HEALTHY NUMBER 6 OVER THERE FLASHIN' ALL THAT BLING? A-HEM.
Keep going, creep! You don't deserve a planet like Earth!
So you're on *his* side?
Calm down, Janet.
I didn't...
HOORAY!
HOORAY!
CLAP CLAP CLAP CLAP CLAP CLAP CLAP CLAP CLAP CLAP CLAP CLAP
The crisis is averted... thanks to *The Avengers!*
Thanks. Thank you. Happy to help.
That's Spider-Man, with a hyphen.
When are we going to tell them that Ego really left because he thought our planet gave him cooties?
Oh... **never.**
OUR HEROES
The End